JASON ROBERTSON

HOCKEY SUPERSTAR

BY ROY RATHBURN

Book design by Jake Nordby
Cover design by Jake Nordby

Photographs ©: Tony Gutierrez/AP Images, cover, 1, 4, 22–23, 30; Brandon Wade/AP Images, 7; Kevin Light/Getty Images Sport/Getty Images, 8; Christopher Szagola/Cal Sport Media/AP Images, 10–11; Bruce Bennett/Getty Images Sport/Getty Images, 12; Vaughn Ridley/Getty Images Sport/Getty Images, 14–15; John Rivera/Icon Sportswire/AP Images, 16–17; Jonathan Daniel/Getty Images Sport/Getty Images, 19; John Woods/The Canadian Press/AP Images, 20–21; Emil T. Lippe/AP Images, 24; Ethan Miller/Getty Images Sport/Getty Images, 27; Red Line Editorial, 29

Press Box Books, an imprint of Press Room Editions, Inc.

ISBN
978-1-63494-875-3 (library bound)
978-1-63494-893-7 (paperback)
978-1-63494-927-9 (epub)
978-1-63494-911-8 (hosted ebook)

Library of Congress Control Number: 2023922357

Distributed by North Star Editions, Inc.
2297 Waters Drive
Mendota Heights, MN 55120
www.northstareditions.com

Printed in the United States of America
082024

About the Author

Roy Rathburn is a retired English teacher and former hockey player, coach, and official, from northern Minnesota.

TABLE OF CONTENTS

ENERGY TRANSFER
CCM
21
CCM
21
CCM
CCM
CCM

1 RIGHT PLACE, RIGHT TIME

Jason Robertson waited just outside the face-off circle. He stood in front of the goalie in the Columbus Blue Jackets defensive zone. Robertson watched the puck drop as his Dallas Stars won the face-off.

Robertson skated back toward the blue line. The winger curled around as he saw teammate Jani Hakanpää start to fire a shot. A true goal-scorer knows to skate where the puck is going, not where it has

Jason Robertson's first-period goal against the Blue Jackets was his sixth of the 2021–22 season.

been. So, Robertson started to dart toward the goal.

He was in the right place at the right time. The Columbus goalie blocked Hakanpää's shot. But the puck dropped right into Robertson's path. The goalie didn't have time to cover the net as Robertson fired home a goal. Dallas had jumped out to a 1–0 lead just 68 seconds into the game.

The game was tied 2–2 with 2:50 left in the second period. Dallas center Joe Pavelski beat a Columbus defender with a fancy deke. He had Robertson to his left as he raced in on goal. Pavelski hit him with a pass, and Robertson did the rest.

DOING WORK EARLY

Jason Robertson's early goal continued a trend for the 2021–22 Dallas Stars. It was the fourth time in a row the Stars had scored within the first 75 seconds of a game. That was the longest streak in NHL history. The streak ended with their next game.

Robertson celebrates his game-winning goal against the Blue Jackets.

He picked out his target and fired a rocket through the goalie's legs.

Robertson's goal proved to be the winner in a 3–2 victory. It was a team effort. But the pure goal-scoring of Robertson was the extra boost this young Stars team needed.

USA
BAUER
15
CCM

2 MOVING NORTH

Los Angeles doesn't produce many National Hockey League (NHL) players. Hockey isn't the most popular sport in California. But for Jason Robertson, it was a hockey paradise.

Jason was born in Arcadia, California, on July 22, 1999. His family had season tickets to the Los Angeles Kings. Jason and his brothers loved watching their NHL heroes up close. And regularly watching the best players in the world inspired them to play hockey themselves.

Jason Robertson tallied seven points in seven games during the 2019 World Junior Championship.

While Los Angeles was great for pro hockey, there were fewer opportunities for youth players. As Jason improved his skills, he started playing in better leagues. But he had to travel long distances to play in those games. When Jason was 10, his family decided to move to Michigan to give him more hockey opportunities.

From a young age, Jason played a balanced game. He scored goals at will. He could also set up teammates to score. As he grew, Jason developed good strength and size. After dominating Michigan's youth leagues, Jason chose to go to Canada to play junior hockey.

Jason played for the Kingston Frontenacs of the Ontario Hockey League (OHL). Many NHL

In 2016, Jason Robertson played in a game with the best US hockey prospects.

USA HOCKEY
CCM
All-American
PROSPECTS
GAME
Philadelphia, Pennsylvania
Reebok

Jason Robertson was the seventh American taken in the 2017 NHL Entry Draft.

players start out in the OHL. And Jason made the Frontenacs at the age of 16. That was the youngest age allowed for an OHL player.

Despite his age, Jason recorded 18 goals and 14 assists. The next year, Jason became the focus of the team's scoring attack. He exploded for 42 goals and 39 assists.

Jason scored nearly a quarter of Kingston's goals by himself.

Not surprisingly, NHL teams took notice. But some teams worried that Jason's skating ability wasn't good enough for the NHL. Also, Jason was still young. He needed more time to develop.

There was at least one team willing to take a chance on him. The Dallas Stars selected Jason 39th overall in the 2017 NHL Entry Draft. The Stars believed in Jason's potential. Now it was up to him to show if he could live up to the expectations.

A ROLE MODEL

Jason Robertson's mother, Mercedes, was born in the Philippines. As a kid in Southern California, Jason often saw other Asian American hockey players. But players of Asian descent are still rare in the NHL. Jason became just the third Filipino player in league history. He enjoys being someone to look up to for the next generation of Asian American players.

CCM
OHL
K
TRIGGER

3 THE LONG ROAD TO DALLAS

The Stars felt lucky to get a player like Jason Robertson. But they knew he wasn't ready for the NHL. So Robertson stayed with the Frontenacs, where he had been named an assistant captain.

Robertson produced in another fine season. He scored 87 points and added 18 more in the playoffs. Meanwhile, Robertson stayed in touch with the Stars' development staff. He kept working on his skating with the hope of playing in the NHL.

Robertson played for the Frontenacs for four seasons from 2015-16 to 2018-19.

CCM
18
CCM

After the OHL season, Robertson signed a contract with the Stars. Dallas assigned him to its minor league team, the Texas Stars. Robertson practiced with the team as it prepared for the playoffs. But he struggled to keep up with the speed of the older, stronger players.

Robertson worked hard for one more OHL season. After a strong start with the Frontenacs, the team traded him to the Niagara IceDogs. Robertson reached new heights, recording 79 points in only 38 games with Niagara.

Robertson's production with the IceDogs impressed Dallas. The team sent him back to the Texas Stars to see if he belonged. Robertson showed that he did, scoring

Robertson played a total of 60 games for the Texas Stars.

13 goals and adding 12 assists in 39 games. He played so well that Dallas called him up on February 13, 2020, to make his NHL debut.

Robertson played in only three NHL games that season. But he proved he was in the mix for an NHL spot the next season. A few Stars players suffered injuries and illness in 2020–21. That opened a spot on the team's fourth forward line. From there, Robertson would have to work his way up.

Robertson didn't play much early on. And when he did play, he struggled with his confidence. He was afraid to make mistakes. However, he listened to his

THE BROTHERS ROBERTSON

Jason Robertson is not the only NHL player in his family. The Toronto Maple Leafs drafted his brother Nicholas in 2019. Nicholas made his NHL debut during Toronto's 2020 playoff run. At just 18 years old, he became the youngest player to debut in the playoffs since the 1990s.

Robertson celebrates a game-winning goal against the Chicago Blackhawks in 2021.

coaches. He put in extra time to work on his strength and skating.

Robertson scored his first NHL goal on February 7, 2021. By the end of April, he led the team with 15 goals and 40 points. He ended up finishing second in Rookie of the Year voting. The hard work was finally paying off.

HAT TRICK HERO

Jason Robertson capped off his first NHL hat trick in a thrilling way. With less than 40 seconds to go in overtime, Robertson outskated a Winnipeg Jets defender to gain control of a loose puck. The defender tripped Robertson with his stick. But Robertson still scored to secure the win for the Stars.

7-ELEVEN

ENERGY TRANSFER
CCM
21
DALLAS STARS
Dr Pepper

4 BECOMING A STAR

By the 2021–22 season, the days of Robertson playing on the Stars' fourth line were long gone. Robertson played enough to earn a spot on the team's top line. He joined left winger Roope Hintz and veteran superstar Joe Pavelski.

Robertson's line powered the Stars to a great season. On March 4, 2022, Robertson scored his first career hat trick. In Dallas's next game, he recorded another hat trick. Those six goals were among 41 Robertson scored that season.

Robertson's 11 game-winning goals in the 2021–22 season were the most in the NHL.

Joe Pavelski (left), Roope Hintz (24), and Robertson (21) combined to score 261 points in the 2022–23 season.

Few players in team history had reached that mark.

After barely missing out on the playoffs the year before, the Stars secured a spot in 2022. But Robertson wasn't able to score at his regular-season pace. His coach even took him off the top line in Game 4 of the opening round. He recorded one goal and three assists in the series. The Stars lost to the Calgary Flames in seven games.

After a full year of experience playing together, Robertson, Hintz, and Pavelski were back on the same line in 2022–23. And they were better than ever. Robertson was by far the team's top offensive player. He set new career highs with 46 goals and 63 assists. For the first time, Robertson played in the NHL All-Star Game.

The Stars rolled into the 2023 playoffs as one of the

BEST IN BIG D

Robertson tallied 109 points in 2022–23. That was the second-most in Stars history. The record holder was Bobby Smith. He scored 114 points in 1981–82 when the team played in Minnesota. The Stars moved to Dallas in 1993. Since then, no player other than Robertson had scored more than 93.

NHL's top teams. Robertson delivered under pressure this time. He scored a goal in Game 1 of the first round. That goal kicked off a much stronger playoff performance for Robertson. He tallied 18 points in 19 postseason games. Robertson's play helped the Stars reach the Western Conference Finals. In that series, he scored five goals in six games. However, the Stars fell to the Vegas Golden Knights.

The Stars were a young, exciting, high-scoring team. And Robertson was at the center of it. It took a lot of hard work to get there, but Robertson developed into the team's brightest star. Dallas fans hoped he could shine even brighter.

Robertson celebrates one of his five goals in the 2023 Western Conference Finals.

EXIT
MARTINEZ
23
33
AN RBC
TRUE

TIMELINE

1. **Arcadia, California (July 22, 1999)**
   Jason Robertson is born.

2. **Northville, Michigan (2009)**
   The Robertson family moves to Michigan for Jason and his brothers to play more competitive hockey.

3. **Kingston, Ontario (April 11, 2015)**
   The Kingston Frontenacs of the Ontario Hockey League select Robertson in the OHL draft. Robertson goes on to play four seasons for Kingston.

4. **Chicago, Illinois (June 24, 2017)**
   The Dallas Stars select Robertson 39th overall in the NHL Entry Draft.

5. **Toronto, Ontario (February 13, 2020)**
   Robertson makes his NHL debut in Toronto against the Maple Leafs.

6. **Dallas, Texas (April 26, 2022)**
   Robertson scores his 40th goal of the 2021–22 season, becoming the fourth player in Dallas history to score 40 or more goals in a season.

7. **Sunrise, Florida (February 4, 2023)**
   Robertson plays in his first NHL All-Star Game.

MAP

1
2
3
4
5
6
7
N

AT A GLANCE

Birth date: July 22, 1999

Birthplace: Arcadia, California

Position: Left wing

Shoots: Left

Size: 6-foot-3 (191 cm), 200 pounds (91 kg)

NHL team: Dallas Stars (2020–)

Previous teams: Texas Stars (2019–20), Niagara IceDogs (2018–19), Kingston Frontenacs (2015–19)

Major awards: NHL All-Star (2023), NHL All-Rookie Team (2021)

Accurate through the 2022–23 season.

GLOSSARY

assists
Passes, rebounds, or deflections that result in goals.

captain
A player who serves as the leader of a team.

debut
First appearance.

deke
A movement faked in a certain direction to confuse an opponent.

draft
An event that allows teams to choose new players coming into the league.

hat trick
When a player scores three or more goals in a game.

junior hockey
A level of hockey in which young players can improve their skills.

line
A set of defensemen or forwards that a player typically is paired with while on the ice.

rookie
A first-year player.

veteran
A player who has spent several years in a league.

TO LEARN MORE

Books

Berglund, Bruce. *Hockey GOATs: The Greatest Athletes of All Time.* North Mankato, MN: Capstone Press, 2024.

Cain, Harold P. *Dallas Stars.* Mendota Heights, MN: Press Room Editions, 2023.

Wiseman, Blaine. *Stanley Cup.* New York: Lightbox Learning, 2024.

More Information

To learn more about Jason Robertson, go to **pressboxbooks.com/AllAccess**.

These links are routinely monitored and updated to provide the most current information available.

INDEX